WHAT HAPPENED TO MR TORTOISE SHELL?

THE STORY OF GREEDY TOITOISE

MIMI EJUS

TABLE OF CONTENTS

Chapter 1

A long time agone when the tortoise and the birds were buddies. A terrible famine hit an ancient animal kingdom. It had not rained for two whole years and all of the crops were dying. The animals hoped and prayed for an end to the terrible drought, but the sky was no longer able to gather enough clouds, and the rains did not come.

Ijapa, the cunning tortoise, lived on the outskirts of the village with his wife. It was proclaimed that there was going to be a big party in heaven and anyone who could fly could attend. When Mr Tortoise heard about this he told Mrs Tortoise that hed like to attend the party but Mrs Tortoise answered him saying, " Why would you want to attend a party thats in heaven? You do n't truly have feathers. How do you plan to get there? " Mr Tortoise thought about this for a while also went back to his woman and told her that hed an idea. " Whats that idea? " Mrs Tortoise asked curiously.

“ Im going to call a meeting and ask all the birds to borrow me a feather each for the party. ” Mrs Tortoise was pretty pleased with his idea. But little did she know that Mr Tortoise had plans other than the one hed told her.

Chapter 2

Mr Tortoise also went on and called a meeting with the birds and reasoned with them for a feather each. After a long time allowing the birds decided to borrow him their feathers. Immediately they gave him their feathers he came up with a new idea telling them that, " When you attend a party you theres a need to get a nick-name which would be called your party name and if you do n't you wont enjoy the party and wont be treated well at the party. The birds agreed since they had noway attended a party formerly and Mr Tortoise was the only one who claimed hed been to a party.

Chapter 3

They all also gave themselves a name and
Mr Tortoise said his party name would be

4 all of you.
When the day of the party came Mr Tortoise
put on his espoused feathers and said good
bye to Mrs Tortoise. Mr Tortoise too soared
into heaven for the party. When they
reached the party they were all asked for
their names and they all gave their party
names rejoicing and thanking Mr Tortoise
for telling them the big party secret.

Chapter 4

The party started with the serving of the foods and drinks and every one was asked to take a seat around the tables. Mr Tortoise made sure he sat among one of the people to around the big table so he sat at the far end of the table. moreover the party waitperson started giving out the food and after kola nuts were presented and eaten, the people of the sky set before their guests; the sweetest dishes Tortoise had ever seen or dreamed of. The soup was brought out hot from the fire and in the same pot in which it had been cooked. It was full of meat and fish. There were pounded yam and also yam pottage cooked with palm oil and fresh fish. There were also pots of palm wine. When everything had been set before the guests, one of the people of the sky came forward and tasted a little from each jar. He then invited the birds to eat. But Tortoise jumped to his feet and asked: "For who has you prepared this feast?"

"For all of you," replied the man.

Tortoise turned to the birds and said, "You remember that my name is All of you. The custom here is to serve the spokesman first and the others later. They will serve you when I have eaten."

He began to eat, and the birds grumbled angrily. The sky's people thought it must be their custom to leave all the food for their King. So Tortoise ate the best part of the food and drank two pots of palm wine so that he was full of food and drink and his body filled out in his shell. Each time she brought the food she said it was for all of you so they passed the food on to Mr Tortoise at the end of the table. This went on and on until the birds started complaining. By then all the food that had been brought was more or less finished by Mr Tortoise.

Chapter 5

The birds noticed that indeed with all the complaining no one was doing anything about it. Mr Tortoise had too much food for just himself and the food was nearly finished. Besides that it was getting late and the party was nearly over. They decided to go to the party organizer and ask what was going on.
The party organizer said to them that they were all supposed to have eaten and be filled with food by then because the food was for all of them. The birds did n't appear to understand so the party organizer told them that when the food was brought out and they were told that it was for everyone of them that mean that they should have shared the food among themselves and not for Mr toitise alone..

Chapter 6

furthermore it came to their knowledge that Mr Tortoise had cheated them because they told the party organizer about the party name and the organizer told them that there was no suchlike thing as a party name and that everyone was treated evenly at a party. They were so angry that they didnt know what to do. So the birds quickly called a quick meeting among them selves. They decided that they will each collect the feathers that they had given to Mr Tortoise and they will each fly back to earth leaving him in heaven but they had to collect their feathers in a way that hed not notice that it was a plan. They thought and thought and thought and they came up with an idea. They took turns to collect their feathers from Mr Tortoise telling him that they wanted it urgently for some thing genuinely important. After they had collected their feathers they told Mr Tortoise that hed deceived them and they were going to pay him back for deceiving them.

Chapter 7

Mr Tortoise knew that he was shamefaced
so he didnt say anything but he just
continues to eat and watch them leave.

When the last person(who was Mr Vulture)
was about to leave he called him back and
asked him if he could do him a favour. Mr
Vulture agreed and asked what the favor
was, he told him that he should please ask
his woman to gather all the soft and sponger
possession they had around there house
and spread them outside their house cause
he was about to jump from heaven and he
wanted to land on soft and sponger
possession so that he does n't break his
body. Mr Vulture replied " yes please,
ofcourse, I will ".

Chapter 8

When he flew back down to earth he told
Mrs Tortoise that Mr Tortoise wanted her to
take out all the hard and wooden things they
had in there house and spread them outside
the house because he wanted to do a stunt
when he is coming down to earth.
Mrs Tortoise thought for a while but since
that was her husbands request she had to
do it. She went into the house and did
exactly what she thought her husband had
asked her to do.

And so she brought out her husband's hoes,
machetes, spears, guns, and even his
cannon.Mr Vulture went back to heaven to
tell Mr Tortoise that his wife had done just
as he had requested.Mr Tortoise thought
that was good news. .Tortoise looked down
from the sky and saw his wife bringing
things out, but it was too far to see what
they were. When all seemed ready, he
immediately jumped down shouting "am
coming"and let himself go. He fell and fell
and fell until he began to fear that he would

never stop falling. And then, like the sound of his cannon, he crashed on the compound.

His shell broke into pieces. Luckily there was a great medicine man in the neighbourhood. Tortoise's wife sent for him, and he gathered all the bits of shell and stuck them together. That is why Tortoise's body is not smooth.
He landed with a great shock on the really hard thing breaking his shell into several pieces. And that is why the Tortoise has a cracked shell up until now.

Lesson learned from the story.

- Don't be greedy.
- Always share what you have with your friends.
- When you think you know better than anyone, always help people out with that knowledge.
- Troubles, challenges and disaster awaits greedy people because they'll surely get into trouble and there will be no one to help them out.